PUFFIN BOC

The Day the Smells
Went Wrong

The Day the Smells Went Wrong

Catherine Sefton

Illustrated by
John Rogan

PUFFIN BOOKS

PUFFIN BOOKS

Published by the Penguin Group
Penguin Books Ltd, 27 Wrights Lane, London W8 5TZ, England
Penguin Books USA Inc., 375 Hudson Street, New York, New York 10014, USA
Penguin Books Australia Ltd, Ringwood, Victoria, Australia
Penguin Books Canada Ltd, 10 Alcorn Avenue, Toronto, Ontario, Canada M4V 3B2
Penguin Books (NZ) Ltd, 182–190 Wairau Road, Auckland 10, New Zealand

Penguin Books Ltd, Registered Offices: Harmondsworth, Middlesex, England

First published by Hamish Hamilton 1988
Published in Puffin Books 1995
5 7 9 10 8 6 4

Text copyright © Catherine Sefton, 1988
Illustrations copyright © John Rogan, 1988
All rights reserved

The moral right of the author and illustrator has been asserted

Made and printed in Belgium by Proost

Jackie and Phil had buttered toast for breakfast.

"Mum?" said Phil. "This toast smells of tar."

"Just eat it!" said Mum, who was flying round collecting baby bits and pushchairs and had no time to talk.

"We don't want to," said Jackie and Phil.

Mum was annoyed, but she hadn't time to fight about it.

"All right," she said. "Leave it."

They piled out of the house in a scurry of schoolbags and pushchairs, and then they had to single file down the pavement outside, where the men were putting fresh tar on the road.

Sniff went Jackie.

Sniff-sniff went Phil.

"That tar smells of toast!" said Phil.

"And our toast smelt of tar!" said Jackie.

"Oh!" said Somebody.

"Did you say 'Oh'?" said Phil to Jackie.

"No, you did!" said Jackie.

They went past the Fruit Shop.

Sniff went Jackie.

Sniff-sniff went Phil.

"Mum, that fruit shop smells of fi . . . "
began Jackie, but Mum grabbed her arm.
They hustled around the corner, past the
Fish Shop.

Fruit and Vegetable Shop.   J. Smith.

Sniff went Jackie.
Sniff-sniff went Phil.

The Fish Shop smelt of apples and
oranges and tomatoes and grapes.
"Oh NO!" said Somebody.
Phil and Jackie looked around, but
there was nobody to be seen.

"In you go!" said Mum. "See you this afternoon!" and she pushed Phil and Jackie through the school gates, and swerved off down the pavement doing fifty miles an hour with the pushchair.

Little Acorn School

"Everything smells wrong this morning!" said Phil, when they got inside the school. "Like this corridor."

Sniff went Jackie.

Sniff-sniff went Phil.

"It ought to smell of polish and chalk," said Phil. "But it doesn't! It smells like . . ."

"... like the swimming-pool!" said Jackie.

They both held their noses, and carried on down to Miss Boot's classroom.

Behind them in the corridor, Somebody said: "Oh! No! O-O-H!"

But nobody heard. Everybody was too busy sniffing and getting confused.

Mr Swift's bicycle smelt of roses and Miss Boot's roses in the classroom smelt of bicycle oil. Miss Boot had put on her new perfume because she was in love with Mr Swift. She wanted him to think she smelt lovely.

"What's that awful cabbage smell, Miss Boot?" Mr Swift said when he met her in the corridor. "Is it our school dinner?"

And poor Miss Boot cried.

"Oh, OOH!" said Somebody.

Things got worse by breaktime.

The teachers' *coffee* smelt of *tea*, and their *tea* smelt of *coffee*, so nobody drank any of it.

Down the corridor, in Miss Boot's
room, everything smelt wrong.

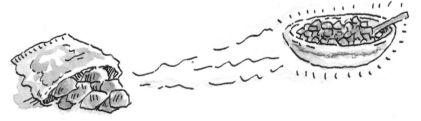

Smoky bacon crisps smelt of cornflakes.

Chocolate smelt of carrots.

And the chalk box smelt of dead
dragons with dirty socks!

"**OOOOOH! NOOOOO!**" said Somebody. "I'll lose my job!"

"Everytime we sniff something that smells wrong, somebody goes 'Oh' or 'Oh no' or says 'I'll lose my job!'," said Jackie.

"It's only me," said the Somebody, sounding very sad.

Jackie and Phil whirled round. There, sitting on top of the Games Box, was the Somebody.

"Sorry," he said. "It's all my fault!"

"Who are you?" said Phil.

"I'm the Chief Inspector of Smells!" said the Somebody. "I fix the smells when they go wrong."

"Do it then!" said Phil and Jackie.

"Can't!" said the Chief Inspector of Smells. "I've lost my Smelling List."

"*Spelling* List?" said Phil.

"SMELLING List," said the Chief Inspector of Smells. "My List of Smells. The smells round here have got all muddled up and I can't put them right without it."

"Where did you lose it?" said Phil.

"Somewhere in this school!" said the Chief Inspector.

"Hunt the Smelling List!" said Jackie.

And Jackie and Phil and the Chief Inspector of Smells dashed about looking for the Smelling List, but they had to stop when the bell went.

They still hadn't found it by lunch-break, and then things got worse.

Nobody wanted to eat mince meat and cabbage with savoury sauce that smelt like Miss Boot's perfume.

"We won't eat that!" all the children cried.

"Quite right, children," said Miss Boot, and she scolded the cook.

"We want our dinners!" shouted all the children who took dinners, and they marched around the school waving banners and flags.

"There's nothing else for it," said Miss Boot. "Clothes pegs on our noses!"

"Miss, Miss!" said Jackie. "We can't do lessons with clothes pegs on our noses!"

"Right, Jackie," said Miss Boot. "I will send for the parents to take you home. We cannot teach with clothes pegs on our noses either."

"No work with pegs on!" cheered all the children.

"Oh yes, there will be!" said Miss Boot,
and she dashed back to the Staff Room,
and came back with an armful of Spelling
Lists.

"One each to everyone in your class,"
she told Phil, and she gave him a pile.

Phil started giving the Spelling Lists out. They were like this:

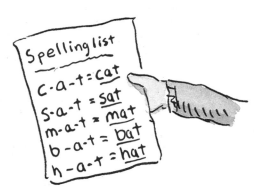

But one wasn't. It was like this:

"Oh!" said Phil, and he stuffed it up his jumper.

"Now go home with your mums and dads!" said Miss Boot.

They all went home, with pegs on their noses. Most of the mums and dads had pegs on their noses too, because there were odd smells about.

Meanwhile, back at the school, the
Chief Inspector of Smells was hard at
work on the Smelling List Phil had
slipped to him.

Soon, chocolate smelt like chocolate and bacon smelt like bacon and bicycles smelt like bicycles and Miss Boot smelt like lavender, which is sweet. She smelt so sweet that Mr Swift married her, almost at once.

By the next morning, everything was all right.

Phil and Jackie came down for breakfast as usual.

"Toast!" said Mum, putting it down on the table.

Sniff went Jackie.

Sniff-sniff went Phil.

And they ate it all up, and had two rounds more, because it smelt so fresh, and buttery, and lovely!

SOS FOR RITA
Hilda Offen

Rita is the youngest in her family and her older brothers and sister give her the most boring things to do. What they don't know is that Rita has another identity: she is also the fabulous Rita the Rescuer!

WHAT STELLA SAW
Wendy Smith

Stella's mum is a fortune teller who always gets things wrong. But when football-mad Stella starts reading tea-leaves, she seems to be right every time! Or is she . . .

THE INCREDIBLE SHRINKING HIPPO
Stephanie Baudet

Simon finds a magic hippopotamus in the garden. It shrinks if anyone says a word meaning "small" and grows again if the word "hippopotamus" is said. Simon loves his new pet, but finds out that it isn't the easiest kind of animal to keep . . .